THIS BOOK BELONGS TO:

____

Made in the USA
Las Vegas, NV
13 December 2023

82686433R10066